I Don't Like Orange!

T0337067

Written by Alice Russ Watson

Illustrated by Jan Smith

Collins

Who's in this story?

Listen and say

Amal

Sara

2 Amal's family has a new house, in a new town.

Amal opens the door. She walks into the house. It's nice.

There are lots of boxes in the new house. Amal is helping.

Amal sees a very big box.

She says, "*Hmmm!* I can make a car."

Amal is going into the garden with her box and her paints, now.

This is Sara.

Sara says, "Hello. I'm Sara.
What's your name?"

Amal says, "Hello. I'm Amal."

Sara says, "What are you doing, Amal?"

Amal says, "I'm painting my new car."

Sara says, "Do you want orange wheels?"

Amal says, "No. I'm painting my car purple."

Sara says, "Do you want an orange stripe?"

Amal says, "No. I don't like orange!
My car is purple."

Amal is painting her car but Sara is sad.

Amal says, "I know!" And she runs into her house.

Amal has got a box for Sara.
Amal says, "Here! You can make
an orange car!"

Sara paints her car orange. She paints a purple stripe.

Amal says, "I like your car! I would like a stripe, too."

Sara asks, "What colour would you like?"
Amal says, "Orange!"

Sara paints an orange stripe on
Amal's car.

They are very happy with their
new cars.

Picture dictionary

Listen and repeat

car

orange

paint

purple

stripe

wheel

1 Look and order the story

2 Listen and say

Collins

Published by Collins
An imprint of HarperCollins*Publishers*
Westerhill Road
Bishopbriggs
Glasgow
G64 2QT

HarperCollins*Publishers*
1st Floor, Watermarque Building
Ringsend Road
Dublin 4
Ireland

William Collins' dream of knowledge for all began with the publication of his first book in 1819.

A self-educated mill worker, he not only enriched millions of lives, but also founded a flourishing publishing house. Today, staying true to this spirit, Collins books are packed with inspiration, innovation and practical expertise. They place you at the centre of a world of possibility and give you exactly what you need to explore it.

© HarperCollins*Publishers* Limited 2020

10 9 8 7 6 5 4 3 2

ISBN 978-0-00-839730-2

Collins® and COBUILD® are registered trademarks of HarperCollins*Publishers* Limited

www.collins.co.uk/elt

British Library Cataloguing in Publication Data

A catalogue record for this publication is available from the British Library.

Author: Alice Russ Watson
Illustrator: Jan Smith (Beehive)
Series editor: Rebecca Adlard
Commissioning editor: Zoë Clarke
Publishing manager: Lisa Todd
Product managers: Jennifer Hall and Caroline Green
In-house editor: Alma Puts Keren
Project manager: Emily Hooton
Editor: Tessie Papadopoulou-Dalton
Proofreaders: Natalie Murray and Michael Lamb
Cover designer: Kevin Robbins
Typesetter: 2Hoots Publishing Services Ltd
Audio produced by id audio, London
Reading guide author: Emma Wilkinson
Production controller: Rachel Weaver
Printed and bound by: GPS Group, Slovenia

Download the audio for this book and a reading guide for parents and teachers at www.collins.co.uk/839730